About the Author

I am originally from Dublin, Ireland – the land of poets! I moved to England in 1977 to join the Army which was controversial at the time, and I lost many friends. Despite a life of many ups and downs I have survived and with the encouragement of my sister and friends, I put pen to paper and have hardly stopped since. At the grand age of sixty-three I am having my first work published. I love reading and writing especially if it takes me away from the everyday. I hope you enjoy reading it as much as I did writing it.

To Jean
Happy Reading
1/7/25

The Haunted House

Ann K. S. Thayre

The Haunted House

Olympia Publishers
London

www.olympiapublishers.com
OLYMPIA PAPERBACK EDITION

A CIP catalogue record for this title is
available from the British Library.

ISBN: 978-1-80439-571-4

This is a work of fiction.
Names, characters, places and incidents originate from the writer's
imagination. Any resemblance to actual persons, living or dead, is
purely coincidental.

First Published in 2024

Olympia Publishers
Tallis House
2 Tallis Street
London
EC4Y 0AB

Printed in Great Britain

Dedication

I dedicate this book to my sister Barbara and to my friends at the Friday health group for encouragement and support given to me to take the step of putting my ideas in writing. Thank you all so much. x

Acknowledgements

I would like to thank my sister Barbara for the endless hours she put in with proofreading and encouraging me to keep going.

It was Mr Murphy who started it all. He ran into the pub one night, having left ten minutes beforehand, looking pale and shaky. He shouted out to anyone who would listen that he had seen a ghost and not only had he seen a ghost, but he had also heard it screaming.

Everyone in the pub laughed; they knew Mr Murphy well and his ability to tell tall tales of witches, ghosts, and lost souls. No one took much notice of him anymore, but we were children at the time and soon these stories started to make an impact on us.

When we heard about this ghost and screaming, we went to investigate. The house stood just back from the road. There was a tall iron gate leading into the garden, and a path to the front door. Although everyone knew the house was empty, our imaginations made us believe that we saw someone in there. We would stand looking and calling for the witch to come out, but of course no one ever did. Sometimes when we were being really daring, we would throw stones at the windows until one day we saw them all boarded up. We tried climbing over the gate but someone had put wire on the top so we couldn't do that. In the end we got bored but Mr Murphy continued with his insistence that he was always seeing the ghost and hearing the scream.

I grew up and moved away from the village. Mr Murphy died taking his stories with him. Occasionally I would return to visit my parents and he would still be a topic of conversation in the pub.

On one such visit I decided to walk back from the pub to my parents' house where I was staying. I took the route past the old house which was now a ruin. I stopped and looked at it and wondered about the people who had lived there and why it had remained empty for so many years. It would have made a beautiful house if it had been looked after. As I stood looking at it in the fading light, I could have sworn I saw something moving through the only window which had lost its boarding. Maybe it was Mr Murphy looking for his ghosts!

I continued home and spoke to my father about the house. Although he had not grown up in the village, he did remember at the time when they moved in there had been people living in it. They had kept themselves to themselves and not had much to do with the village life. He couldn't remember if they had children or not. He did remember when my mother was working in the local village shop for a short time a woman would come in and order a lot of items to be delivered to the house. She had tried to talk to the woman who always kept her head down and said nothing. So, the villagers never knew much about who was in the house or even how long they had been there or when and where they went.

I asked my father what he thought about me buying the house and maybe pulling it down and rebuilding. He thought there would be too much work involved and because of his bad back he would be unable to help me do a lot. My mother of course thought it was a great idea as it would mean that her son would be at home more.

The next day I visited the estate agent in the village. The village had grown over the years and most newcomers referred to it as the town. It was still a pleasant walk from my parent's house to the village and it went past the house giving me a chance to see it in daylight. In the stark brightness of the day, it looked in worse condition and it became obvious that it did need a lot of work. I would of course keep a lot of greenery as I could see an oak tree at the back of the house and there were some beautiful rambling roses. My mother was a keen gardener and surely, she would be able to rescue a lot of the plants. I carried on my walk to the town dreaming of mansions and stables. By the time I had got to the estate agent I had built a palace!

Mr Brooke the estate agent looked at me in astonishment when I said I wanted to purchase the house and the land around it.

'Are you a builder?' he asked.

I shook my head.

He started to laugh. 'Do you know anything about building?' He smirked.

I shrugged my shoulders and said no. He laughed louder. 'Then my boy,' he said, 'you have a hell of a job ahead of you and it is going to cost you a pretty penny.' I assured him I had enough money and time as I had just been made redundant.

He took out the paperwork and told me they had had quite a few people look at the land and the house, but everyone thought there was too much work to be done. Construction firms had wanted to buy the land to build factories, but the planning permission had been denied. The only planning permission that was granted was to build a house which was similar to the one that had been there.

I jokingly said that I didn't want to build another ruin. Mr. Brooks then took on a serious look and asked if I would like to know how much it would cost. I nodded waiting for the bombshell, but he broke into a smile and said you can have it for ten pounds. My face must have looked a picture as the other agents in the room were all grinning.

'Are you sure?' I asked in astonishment.

13

'Yes.' Mr. Brooks replied. It has been on the market for too many years to remember. There is no family, and the council would just like to see it restored to a building that would be easier on the eye than it is now.

I took my wallet out to hand over the ten pounds but of course that wasn't allowed. We had to go through the normal legal route of buying a house and this is where a lot of my money would be going.

When Mr. Brooks got the ball rolling I left the estate agents and stood outside looking around. I decided to visit the pub where over a pint I told the landlady what I intended to do with the house. She laughingly warned me to watch out for the ghosts and the witches Mr Murphy had seen and if I was lucky, I might even see Mr Murphy looking for them!

Mr. Brooks had given me a key for the gate and one for the house. On the way home I decided to go in and have a look. Two pints of ale makes the eyes see things differently and all I could see, as the gate creaked and groaned catching on weeds as I pushed it open, was the palace I had dreamed of earlier.

I stumbled my way up the overgrown pathway to the front door. There was actually no lock on the boarding so I clambered around the back of the house. What remained of the back door was ajar. The boarding had been removed. As I pushed the door open it swung off its hinges. Inside it became very apparent this had been the place for children and maybe squatters to play and live in over the years. There was so much rubbish, and the smell was very overpowering. I heard a noise and looked up. There was no ceiling left to the above floor and part of the roof was missing. I relaxed as I saw some pigeons flying and landing.

It was definite I would have to pull the lot down and start again. There did not seem to be anything solid enough left to rebuild on. Leaving the house, I stood and looked at the garden. Yes, I thought, I must get my mother down here and a professional gardener to remove the plants before building work began.

A week went by, and the paperwork was completed and signed. My mother and a gardener had been and looked at the grounds of the house and marked up everything which needed to be dug out and saved. They also put marks on the trees which were to remain, this included the oak tree and a smaller tree beside it. Although the smaller tree looked like it could do with coming out, I decided to keep it and try to bring more life back to it.

I organised the building firm who came in and were quite pleased. They liked nothing better than demolishing and starting with a clean slate. It always prevented the late discovery of rot under floorboards or finding damp foundations. They could start immediately.

I had had the plans drawn up by a local architect for a two-storey house. Along with the discovery of the drawings of the original building, we were able to design a very similar house whilst at the same time bringing it up to modern standards. The work began.

A couple of weeks later I woke up to the sound of my phone ringing. Looking at the number I could see it was the builders. 'You better get down here fast,' the foreman said. 'We have found something not very pleasant.'

I got there as fast as I could to see the workmen all standing around. 'What is going on?' I asked.

'Take a look,' the foreman replied, 'but I warn you it is quite a shock.' I scrambled over some rubble and looked at the hole in the floor where they were pointing.

There in a row neatly placed were human remains. I counted four. It looked like two were very small children, maybe even babies. I felt my stomach knot, but I also felt curious. Who were they? How long had they been there and most of all who put them there?

I called the police and reported what we had found. We were instructed to leave the site immediately. This we did and it wasn't long before they arrived along with a team of experts. We were informed that the work would have to stop until the investigation was over.

At home I discussed the events with my parents, but we did not come to any conclusions and decided we would have to wait until the police were finished. In the meantime, I did some odd jobs for my parents. I also visited the pub a bit more frequently as it took me past the house where for a few days a tent had been in place over the hole where the bones had been. Rumours were rife in the pub. No one seemed to know if the people had left the house or even if they had been taken out in boxes. Ideas of whom the bones belonged to and why they were there, ranged from sacrifices by witches to the remains of Mr Murphy even though the latter had been buried. I decided to go to the local library and see what I could find out.

Going through all the local history books I did discover that the house had belonged to a couple who had no children. There was a black and white photo of them, and they looked very austere. There was no mention of what they did or who they were and as before the mystery continued.

A week went by, and we were allowed to continue building. The site was cleared, and it wasn't long before the foundations were put in. The builders had used some of the bricks from the old house in different areas to help make it look more authentic and as the first floor went up, I could finally see my vision taking shape. It was then that the builders started to pass comments on things disappearing, tools being moved and a general uneasiness in the house.

I decided to have a look one evening on my way back from the pub. As I entered the house, I had a great feeling of satisfaction that soon I could be living here, if that was what I decided to do. As I moved down the hallway, I thought I heard something and looked up but as there was a ceiling and a roof now, I knew it couldn't be pigeons. I stood and listened but didn't hear anything else. I decided it must have been noise from outside. As I finished looking around, I headed towards the front door but as I went to open it, I heard a noise sounding like a muffled scream. I listened carefully but heard no more. Shaking my head, I headed out. Mr Murphy's stories must have played more on my mind then I knew. I stood at the front gate and looked back at the house. I blinked and stared hard. I could have sworn I saw a movement in one of the upper windows. I stood for a few minutes and decided it must have been a trick of the light as I didn't see it again.

It wasn't long before the carcass became a living environment, and the house was ready to move into. The garden had been cleared and replanted with some of the old plants and some new. While this was happening there had been a storm and the smaller tree next to the oak tree had come halfway down resting against the larger tree. I decided looking at it that it would have to come out. It was too dangerous to leave it. The gardener organised a crane to lift it the rest of the way out. I was watching this when suddenly the gardener put up his hand to stop the crane driver. He climbed down into the hole. Struggling out again he had something in his hand. I couldn't quite see what it was from the kitchen window, so I went out. He handed me a rusty tin which we were unable to open. I took it into the shed and with the help of a chisel and a hacksaw I managed to prise the lid off in bits. There was a packet inside wrapped up in plastic. The plastic did not disintegrate as I opened it. I was disappointed; it looked like a very old book and not a bundle of cash as I had hoped. I carefully opened the book and saw that it seemed to be a record or diary. It was still in very good condition and so I went indoors poured myself a beer sat comfortably and started to read.

Inside the cover of the book, it read *this is the diary of Anne Smith age fourteen and a half in the year 1958.*

I started to read. It wasn't a daily diary it was more like a journal written in very childish handwriting. There seemed to be a date entered here and there but nothing regular.

It began. *My name is Anne Smith I think I am fourteen and a half. I do not know because they won't tell me. I have a younger sister who is thirteen and a half I think. We have never been outside, so we do not know what goes on in the world. Sometimes if we are lucky, we can peep out the window and see people going past. I was asleep when we came to this house, and I cannot remember where we lived before. I am writing this and hope that someday someone will find us and rescue us. We have food but we must work for it by cleaning the house every day from top to bottom. It doesn't matter if it is already clean, we have to still do it. The man and the woman are not very nice. I don't know if they are our mother and father as we are only allowed to call them Sir and Madam. We have had a few toys over the years but not many. We do not have time to play but we do tell each other stories. One day when I was cleaning, I found a magazine and I sneaked it under my apron. My sister Mary and I would read it over and over again. It helped us to make up stories. Another time I found a book. It was a very strange book. It had lots of words and pictures, mainly pictures. We tried to read it and understand it, but we didn't know what some of the words meant and the pictures were very strange.*

January 1959 it is a new year. A very strange thing happened to my sister and me. The Madam said we were grown up now and we were to do everything the Sir told us to do.

I put the book down and went and got another beer. I didn't like the way this was going but I felt compelled to read it. If I was ever to find out who had lived here this may give me a clue.

I continued reading. *Sir came to my room last night and told me to take my nightdress off. He had a strange look on his face and then he told me to lie on the bed. He climbed on top of me, and he hurt me, and it made me scream. I didn't like it but all he said is you are a woman now and you will do anything I say. I didn't understand what he meant or what he was doing.*

I cried myself to sleep. This is happening at least once a week and I now understand the pictures in the book. When I saw Mary crying, I knew that she was now a woman. We stopped looking at the book.

March 1959, I don't know what's happening to Mary. She was being sick today. I wish we could get out of here. I cannot write much as they are watching us most of the time. Sir still comes to our room and sometimes Madam too.

May 1959, I haven't been able to write for a long time. I tried to stop Sir from hurting us and he twisted my arm I was not able to use it for a long time. Mary is getting bigger. She said something is moving in her belly and she doesn't know what it is.

My belly is getting bigger too and it sometimes feels like I have a butterfly in it.

September 1959 They are watching us all the time and they stop talking when we come into the room. It is difficult to work now as my belly is big. Mary is bigger than me and she sleeps more.

October 1959 Mary is really big she cannot do anymore work; Madam is very annoyed. My belly has got very big but I am lucky it doesn't get in the way so I don't get any beatings and I can carry on working. I found another magazine and it seemed to be about babies. We now know that we are going to have a baby, but we don't know how it will get out.

November 1959 I can hear Mary screaming. They have taken her out of the bedroom and locked me in. The screaming went on for a while and then it was quiet. Suddenly I heard a cry like an animal and then silence. I waited for Mary to come back but she never did. When I asked what had happened to her, they told me it was none of my business. I miss Mary. It is very lonely without her.

December 1959 It is very cold. Mary has not come back. My belly is huge I can feel the baby moving. Sometimes I see something poking out of my belly and when I feel it, it feels like a foot or a hand. Because I am lonely, I talk to the baby. I have been getting pains for a few hours now. I am afraid to tell Sir and Madam. I saw them in the garden yesterday planting a tree. It was very small. I think I will try and get out in the garden and hide this book under the tree because I think when the baby comes, I might have to go away like Mary.

December 1959 The next day. I am still getting pains, but I can still work. They said they are going out today and I was to stay in my room. I had hidden the key so they could not lock me in. I will go into the garden and try to dig a hole to put this book in. Maybe I will come back for it one day. The end, goodbye.

There were no more entries and I felt extremely sad. It now became obvious that the bodies we found were of the two girls and their babies. It also explained the screams that Mr Murphy had heard and no doubt the glimpses of shadows were the girls.

I gave the book to the police. I went to see the vicar of the local church and asked if the bones could be buried in the churchyard now that we had names. Although it would never be known if the girls had been baptised, he agreed to a grave in the corner under a tree.

A few weeks later I stood looking at the headstone which read Anne and Mary Smith, sisters in life, sisters in death and their two unnamed babies. We could only guess what ages they had been when they died and put them as aged fifteen and fourteen. We could not find any records about them.

Despite the burial I knew they were not totally at peace as I still heard a lot of noises in the house and occasionally, I hear crying.

One evening when my parents visited, we decided that we should consult a psychic. I didn't want the girls' ghosts to be banned from the house. I just wanted them to be at peace and maybe even to carry on living there. We consulted a psychic in the next town, and she agreed to help.

When I took her into the house she shivered. She said there was a lot of pain in the house, but she would try to ease that pain. I gave her the instructions and the words I wanted her to use and watched as she moved around the house. I could hear her mumbling Anne and Mary you are safe now you can rest you can play you can run around in this house. It is not the same house. It is a much more loving house, and you will be welcome to stay if or as long as you want.

The psychic said this in every room of the house. There was no response, no cupboard doors swinging open or things flying around the room, just silence when she finished. I would have to wait to see if it worked.

Later that evening I was sitting by the fire having a whiskey and I thought about the room upstairs. I had taken the bed out and put in two armchairs. I had been to the toy shop in the village and purchased toys and books, paper and pencils and anything I could think of to suit two girls. I also put in the room two baby cots with blankets and baby rattles. I had also included a dolls house which had been my mother's.

The fire crackled and I felt warm and contented, satisfied with the day's work. I must have dozed off when something woke me. I heard a giggle. Was it my imagination? I headed towards the stairs. I crept slowly up towards the bedroom and when I opened the door, I noticed the toys had been moved. The figures in the doll's house were in different rooms and a book lay open on the floor. The blankets in the cots were turned back and a rattle lay on a chair. The big difference was the room felt warm. I left it and went back downstairs and once again sat looking at the fire. Occasionally I could hear footsteps and sometimes laughter.

A month went by, and the house continued to feel warm and happy. My guests were very well behaved and although they never answered, I would often sit in the room and read them a story.

Where the tree had stood in the garden, I planted a rose bush and put a little plaque on it with the girls' names on it. On the day I did this I stood looking back at the house. I saw two figures at the window waving at me. They were holding bundles in their arms. The smiles they gave me left me in no doubt they were at peace now in a happy haunted house.

Time went on and I settled into a routine: - visiting the village pub, visiting parents, and reading stories to ghosts. Of course, I never told anyone outside of my parents that I was doing this, or they would have thought I was mad.

We had a new addition to the house. One morning I opened the back door and a black cat walked in. Watching it go towards the hall I followed it. It climbed the stairs and sat outside the door of what I now called the girl's room. Letting it in, it jumped up on one of the chairs and went to sleep.

Thinking it would come down eventually and leave to go back to where it came from, I left it sleeping. I felt a strange feeling as though the house was complete. The cat never left, only going outside for a short time, bringing back a dead mouse or slowworm and depositing these in the bedroom. It spent all the time in that room and so I let it stay. I just called it cat.

I had been in the house a couple of months when a hinge came loose on one of the cupboards in the kitchen. I hadn't invested in any tools, so I went to the shed to see if there were any screwdrivers there.

The shed was concrete and did not have a floor only soil. As I was searching, I made a note to myself that it should be cleared out and a floor put in. At last, finding a small screwdriver I went back to the kitchen to fix the door. The door was very heavy, and it was proving extremely difficult to hold it in place. Suddenly, I felt the weight ease and the door was being held up. I quickly screwed the screws in and shut the door. Hearing a little giggle, I thanked my ghosts. This was the first time they had ventured down while I was in the house, and I could see now why. The cat wanted to go out. Was this the start of them wanting more contact and feeling safe to do so? Who knows what ghosts think.

The next day I headed to the shed and began to clear it. The builders had left some bits behind including a mask which was a bonus as everything was so dusty and dirty.

After an hour I had different piles of items in the garden to be taken to the tip, I also managed to find some workable tools but most of them were broken or too rusty to be of use. Following a short rest for a coffee I tackled the furthest corner of the shed. It wasn't a big shed but as it became less cluttered, I could see potential. In the corner was something covered in a very heavy tarpaulin. I dragged it off in a cloud of dust, dirt, spiders and who knows what else as I was coughing and sneezing. Dragging it outside I dumped it on the lawn. While taking deep breaths I watched spiders scuttle away at high speed. Going back to the shed I could see it had been covering an old writing desk.

I heard a little sneeze which made me nearly pass out with fright. Looking around I spotted the cat sitting in the doorway watching me. I felt a shiver down my spine without knowing why.

Turning back to the desk I began to open the drawers. I was amazed to find papers, pens, magazines. I looked at the date on the magazine and it was 1960. Working out the dates, I found it was fifty-four years old. Amazingly it was in excellent condition, and I began to feel excited that this desk may reveal some history on the house. I retrieved some dusters and a box from the house and dusting off the papers as best I could, I stacked them in the box. I also found a tin box which like the one in the garden was firmly shut, only this time it had a lock. I was feeling more excited by the minute at all the finds.

However, I was also determined to get the shed empty so I could start levelling the ground and concreting it over. Another couple of hours went by and finally the shed was empty.

Fetching a beer, I stood looking at the floor of the shed trying to decide what was the best way to start or which end to start at. The cat had never left the vicinity and now it came and sat beside me. Man and cat looking at soil, wasn't it usually man and dog? It didn't matter because at that moment the cat moved to the far wall of the shed and began to scratch at the ground. I watched him while I drank thinking that he had found a worm or spider. As the cat became more frantic digging at speed I went to investigate. I searched the ground but could not see anything that the cat would want but now it was crying up at me in a terrible howl. The cries were very earie, so I started to scrape with my foot. Nothing was revealed but the cat was becoming more and more noisy and frantically scratching around the area. I left it and fetched a shovel. As I came back in the door of the shed, I stopped in my tracks. The cat had scraped out an outline in the soil and was sitting in the middle of it howling.

I quickly began to work and as I did the cat retreated to the doorway and sat quietly watching me. I had no idea what I was supposed to be looking for but at least the cat was quiet. I had gone down a few inches and decided that I was an idiot, I wasn't finding anything. I put the shovel down and the cat immediately began its howling again.

I picked up the shovel and began digging again. I had switched my mind off thinking of other things when a screech from the cat brought me back down to earth literally. The ground had given way and I had dropped a few more inches. Trying to lift my feet back out of the hole what looked like a skeleton hand came with them. I panicked and clambered out. The hole wasn't very deep but reaching down and brushing soil away I found that the hand was attached to an arm. The cat came and looked, gave a meow and went back to the house.

I stood looking at the hand and arm for a few minutes before pulling myself together and phoning the police. By this time, it was getting dark and they said they would come in the morning. In the meantime, I shut the door and headed indoors.

I didn't feel hungry but made a sandwich, grabbed a beer, and settled at the kitchen table with the box of papers in front of me. The cat had eaten and gone back to the bedroom with the girls.

The house was unusually quiet, and I could hear the clock ticking. Turning on the radio, I settled into an evening of research.

I was disappointed, expecting to find birth certificates or marriage certificates. All there was, were some old newspapers, receipts house sale details and a train times schedule.

I was about to throw the lot in the bin when something urged me to read more. In the train times I found a ring around a town which was about twenty miles away and a ring around the village. Could it be possible the people had come from that town? I began to feel some excitement. Grabbing a sheet of paper, I began to make notes of what I was finding.

Next, I checked the newspapers. This took a long time as I wanted to make sure I did not miss anything. It was fascinating to read of things that happened in the world back then. As I waded through the first one, I found a small article which was circled.

'Middle aged couple die in house fire. The cause of the fire is unknown. Names are being withheld while relatives are contacted.'

Now why was that circled? I noted it down and carried on.

In the second paper I found another article with a ring around it.

Couple who died in house fire named as Patricia and Robert Harris. They leave behind one daughter Mary. Cause of fire is still unknown but as investigations continue a source informed this newspaper that it was thought to be suspicious.

My heart leapt. 'Mary' that was the name of one of my ghosts. Could it be. Could this have been the austere woman in the photograph. With shaking hands, I began to scan the next newspaper.

On the second page there it was in big bold letters.

CAUSE OF FIRE REVEALED

The fire which killed Patricia and Robert Harris in their home on The Green has been declared arson. Police are searching for the daughter Mary who has not been seen since. It is thought she has left the country with her boyfriend and a lot of cash from her parents safe. Anyone with any information should call police on ... ' and there was a phone number.

And there beside the article was the same picture as the one I had found in the library.

I quickly read through the last newspaper but there was nothing more about the fire. The only thing ringed was the advert for this house for sale.

My head was reeling. Could I be getting closer to their identities? I looked at the clock one am, but I couldn't stop now. I made a mug of strong coffee, walked around the kitchen to stretch my legs and then began again.

My notes made, I put the papers to one side. I had put post it notes on them to indicate the pages with the information. Deciding now that the receipts must be important, I began scrutinizing them. Some of them were unreadable with the ink faded. Those that I could read revealed that children's footwear and clothes had been bought. There was a very old receipt for baby milk. The rest were of normal food shopping.

The papers on the sale of the house were more revealing. They had been signed by a Mrs Mary Smith and a Mr Horatio Smith. I let out a gasp. This had to be them. It couldn't be a coincidence that the child had the same name as the woman.

The papers didn't throw out any more information so I started on the tin box.

Squirting some oil in the lock I tried every key I had found in the shed but nothing fit. I couldn't wait until morning to buy something to break the lock so I rang my father.

He was not pleased to be woken in the middle of the night but when I explained all I had found he immediately said he would be over with some tools.

Making fresh coffee I waited. He arrived a short while later with bolt cutters and wrenches and various other items. The bolt cutters broke it first time and we held our breaths as we opened the box.

My legs almost gave way when there on the top I saw a photo of the austere couple and two girls. I dropped into my chair and with shaking hands I lifted the photo out. Turning it over I saw written Mary, Horatio and their two girls Mary and Anne. There wasn't a date which was unusual but the girls looked about seven or eight so it must have been middle fifties. It didn't matter, I thought I had found my answer. Looking through the rest of the box I found a wedding ring which had Patricia and Robert inscribed on the bezzle, the couple who had died in the fire. It was beginning to seem very likely that the daughter and husband had been responsible for the fire which had killed her parents.

My father and I discussed my findings until dawn broke and we could hear the dawn chorus. The cat appeared in the kitchen and jumped on my lap. Sniffing at the box in front of me it hissed and spat then jumped down. I asked my father if he would accompany me up to the girl's room as I would like to see if there would be any reaction to the photo. I made an enlarged copy of the photo, and we headed up. I did not know what to expect, even if they would be able to see it, or if I would be able to see their reaction.

The cat ran ahead of us into the room. with encouragement from my father, I called out to my ghosts. There was no response, so I held the picture up and asked if they knew who the people were and if they were their parents. For a while there was only silence and then a piercing scream filled the air. We had to cover our ears and I let the picture drop to the floor. The cat leapt to the floor and began to spit and hiss at the picture. The screaming went on and on for what felt like forever when suddenly it stopped. We dropped our hands from our ears and listened to complete silence, even the cat had gone back to the chair. I bent down to pick up the picture when it suddenly lifted in the air and was torn in half.

I wanted to be sure so I asked the girls if it was their parents could they rip the picture up some more. Very slowly the picture was torn again and again into small pieces. We had our confirmation. Picking up the bits of paper we left the room.

Despite it being so early in the morning my father poured us both a whisky and we sat discussing what to do next. The answer came with a knock to the door.

The police and forensics had arrived. I led them round the side of the house to the shed. Leaving them to it I went back into the kitchen to make breakfast. We decided not to mention the ghosts to the police, after all it was just a bit possible, they wouldn't believe us.

We had just finished our bacon and eggs when the police inspector came into the kitchen.

'Do you have a black cat?' he asked. I nodded.

'Very strange. He is sitting watching us and won't budge. Every time we expose a bit more of the skeleton he howls. It is beginning to spook us.'

I smiled and told him not to worry, that animals behaved very strangely around dead bodies.

He sat down and I poured him a coffee. I then decided to tell him what I had found. To say he was delighted would be an understatement. I heard him mutter about promotion. It didn't matter that I had found all the clues and evidence, he would be taking the credit. At least he could claim it for the solving of the fire murders and the identity of the bones found under the floorboards, but the identity of the body and whereabouts of Mary Smith were yet to be resolved.

He wanted all the papers but before I handed them over, I made copies of everything. I was determined to find what had happened to Mary and Horatio Smith. I was also thinking that when I did find out would my ghosts leave me. I had become accustomed to them being around; I would hate for them to go and if they did would the cat go too.

The inspector went back to work and my father went home. I sat in an armchair and dosed off.

I was in the middle of a nightmare of a skeleton chasing me and about to strangle me when I was shook awake. Jumping up in fright I almost knocked over a member of the forensic team.

'We are finished now and have removed the body. It appears to be that of a male, but we are unable to confirm until we have done a proper examination back at the lab. While the investigation is being carried out can you refrain from going into the shed and don't let that cat in there again.'

I agreed and he left. Suddenly the cat appeared and whined to get out. Watching it go towards the shed I wondered what it would do. It began scratching at the door. Deciding that as it had already been inside numerous times it couldn't do any more harm. I opened the door to let it in. It went over to where the body had been and sniffed around. This time there was no howling. It came back to me and rubbed against my legs before heading down the garden. Was he leaving now the body was found?

Looking around the shed I shivered and closed the door. Another decision I would have to make was as to whether I would keep the shed or knock it down. How much would it affect me knowing a body had been there. Sometimes imagination was not a good thing.

With nothing more to be done I made some dinner and settled in front of the fire. There were no noises from upstairs and I felt lonely. I was so used to them by now. A scratching at the door told me the cat had come back and I let it in. This time it came and sat on my lap. When I went upstairs to bed, I was relieved to see it go into the girl's room and hear a giggle.

The next day was a Monday, so I headed out to the town twenty miles away to try and find the area where the house had been burned down.

It didn't take long to get there and find The Green. It was in fact an area of grass surrounded by a few houses. I got out of my car and wandered around looking at each house trying to work out if any of them had had a fire.

I supposed I shouldn't have been surprised when a police car pulled up beside me. I had seen some curtains twitching.

'Excuse me sir, can I help you with anything?' A young

female police officer had got out of the car and was standing in front of me.

'Actually, yes, you can. I'm looking for the house that was in a fire back in the fifties and two people died. You are too young to have been around, but do you know which one it was.'

She pointed to a piece of wasteland at the end of the row of houses.

'It stood there. I heard the fire was so fierce there was nothing left, and the remains were pulled down.'

'Do you know if the daughter was ever found?'

She shook her head. 'I would have to look up the case files as it was before my time. What do you want to know for?'

I didn't know how much to tell her, so I just told her everything I had told the police inspector and about the bones of the children.

She shook her head sadly and said I could come back to the station with her and she would try to find the old files.

The police station wasn't that far and when she had put in a request for any files pertaining to the fire, we headed to the canteen.

The smell of food reminded me I hadn't had any breakfast. I had been so eager to get going I only paused long enough to feed the cat.

She waited patiently with her hands round a mug of coffee while I tucked into a late breakfast of egg and bacon. When I had finished eating and in between sips of coffee I told her the story of buying the house and the discovery of the bones of the children. She was intrigued and didn't say much. I felt a bit stupid telling her about the ghost stories, but she seemed to accept that that was all they were, stories.

When we had almost finished our second coffee, she got a

call to say the files had been put on her desk. With rising excitement and apprehension, I followed her to her desk which was in a large office. Desks were piled high with files and phones were ringing. Going towards her desk I felt a wave of disappointment when I saw that the file was very thin.

She also sounded disappointed as she opened the file and began reading. All that was in it was what I already knew. The fire had killed two people and the daughter was missing. The last sighting of her had been boarding a train. They did not have all the CCTV in those days so no more sightings had been reported. I asked if I could just sit for a while and read it through.

The police officer sat back and left me to read the file. There had to be something in here to give me some clues. No matter how many times I read it there was nothing. Even though the file had remained open nothing had been added since the original investigation.

I thanked the officer and wished her a good day. Leaving the station, I felt defeated and headed home.

When I arrived home, there was a message on the answering machine asking me to telephone the inspector.

The phone rang for a while before he answered, and I waited with bated breath for some good news. Once he knew who I was he began

'The body is male. There are no indications of foul play, no broken bones, no bullet holes so it appears the logical explanation would be poison. This would tie in what we used to call a murder by a woman as they liked to use poison. We have no way of identifying him, but we can assume he is the Horatio in the photo. If he is, then where is she? She could also be dead and if not, she must be very old. Anyway, we will try and investigate more but I cannot promise anything.' I thanked him and we hung up.

Feeling I was being watched I turned and saw the cat sitting looking at me.

'OK, OK' I said to him. 'I will keep looking.' He came and rubbed against my legs before disappearing back upstairs again. Not only was I talking to ghosts, but I was also now speaking to the cat as though it was human, I felt I was going mad.

Making a hot drink I gathered my notes and papers and sat in front of the fire going through them again.

Getting clean paper, I began to write down what I had learned so far.

Patricia and Robert Harris – parents of Mary Harris died in a fire.

Mary Harris disappeared believed to have started the fire.

Mary shows up in a photo with a man named Horatio Smith. (I knew the surname from Anne Smiths journal/diary)

Mary and Horatio had two children Mary and Anne. It is assumed that they killed the girls after subjecting them to horrendous treatment.

Horatio – body in shed could be him which leaves the question Where is Mary?

Sitting back something the inspector had said was niggling me. I wish I could remember what it was. I kept going over the notes and then like a flash of lightening it came to me. He had said that if she was still alive, she would be very old by now.

I felt the excitement rising again and wondered how longer I could cope with the roller coaster of ups and downs.

I worked out from the few dates that I had that if alive she could be in her nineties or even a hundred. The excitement left. What were the chances of her still being alive.

Rising I went and made a sandwich and took a walk around the house to stretch my legs. The girl's room was quiet and I wondered if they were waiting for me to complete the puzzle. The cat raised its head and stretched a paw out to me. I stroked him and felt better. I wasn't on my own I would get to the bottom of this.

Heading back downstairs I decided to phone my parents. My father after a quick hello passed the phone to my mother who proceeded to give me all the gossip from the village. I didn't know who she was talking about and my mind drifted while I just answered with a grunt. Suddenly I was snapped out of it.

'What was that you said, Mum?'

'What about?'

'I don't know the last thing you said about a Mrs something or other and a fall.'

'Well dear you probably don't know her. It's a Mrs Dalton. She is ninety-eight and had been living in the cottage at the end of the back lane. She fell over her front doorstep and broke a hip. The family took the chance to get her into a care home as she was too frail to...'

'That's it, that's it. Thanks, Mum.' I hung up before she could say anymore.

A care home. What if Mary Smith was in one or had been in one? It was getting late so I decided to leave it until morning.

The following day dawned bright and cheerful. I was feeling positive. Finishing breakfast, I switched on my computer and began trawling through the nursing homes in the area. I included all the ones in the surrounding towns.

Looking at the list I was amazed to see so many. Thinking that if I rang them it might be taken as a joke asking for a Mary Smith, I made the decision to go in person. I put together some sandwiches filled a couple of flasks and bottles of water and headed out on my search. I also took the photo with me just in case someone would recognise her. I did not hold much hope on the latter.

I was three hours into my search and feeling quite tired and a bit desponded. No one had heard of her or recognised the photo. Sitting in the car drinking yet another coffee and eating my cheese and pickle sandwich, I began to think that it was a waste of time. Watching people walking by I was asking myself why I was doing this and what was it all for when I nearly had a heart attack as a black streak jumped into the passenger seat and there was the cat watching me. Wiping the coffee off my jeans and retrieving my sandwich from the floor I glared at the cat and began to tell it off. As I was shouting at him, he was purring and patting his paw on my list of homes. There was a rap on the window. 'Yes,' I shouted, turning at the same time to see a police officer standing there. The window was open so I quickly took a breath to calm down and said sorry.

'Are you all right, sir?'

'Yes. I was only shouting at my cat for making me spill my coffee.'

'What cat? he asked sticking his head in the window.

'That cat.' I pointed but the cat wasn't there.

Now where did it go? I searched the car, but it was gone.

The police officer looked at me sceptically and I quickly came up with

'I was rehearsing my lines for a play.'

'If you're sure you are OK. Just take care. Drive safely.' He carried on with his beat.

Putting my head back I closed my eyes and thought I must be losing my mind. But how to explain me spilling coffee, maybe I had dozed off and not realised it. Yes, that was it.

Feeling better I picked up my list and checked the next name on it. It was not far away but as I began to put the list back down, I noticed a tiny tear underneath one of the names.

'The peaceful Orchard' It was a private nursing home about fifteen miles away.

Why not I thought. If the cat had been here, he had left me a sign.

Putting the car in gear I headed off. The traffic was heavy and there seemed to be roadworks on every street. I was becoming very impatient when at last I turned into a residential street. Thinking I had taken a wrong turning I continued and eventually saw the sign for The Peaceful Orchard. Pulling into the driveway I parked the car. It looked a very upmarket home from the outside with beautiful gardens surrounding it. Lots of benches were spread around and a few people were sitting making the most of the sunshine.

Going up the steps I entered a large hallway and wondered if it had been an old house converted. A nurse pointed me towards reception where I found a woman who looked like she was in her fifties. This could be promising.

I put the letter the police inspector had written for me stating that I was working with them. It was beginning to look a bit tatty by now but the receptionist acknowledged it and asked how she could help.

I explained I was looking for a Mary Smith (I was sure I saw her lips twitch) I explained it was genuine not a joke. I showed her the photo and she stared at it for a while.

'Wait here.' She went away taking the photo with her.

I looked around the hall. It was huge with enormous portraits hanging on the walls. I was trying to read the names when she returned.

Walking beside her was a woman who looked like she had

been working in the kitchen. She had flour on her face and her apron was covered in it.

The receptionist introduced her as Mrs Brown who had been a cook in the kitchen for thirty years. The receptionist had only just started and although she could confirm there was a resident by the name of Mary Smith, she did not recognise the photo but the cook did. I looked at the cook with a rising hope.

'Is she the one, the one that is here?'

Mrs Brown studied the photo and said she remembered her arriving at the home.

'Well Sir. It was like this. One day a woman, her, (pointing at the photo) came running into the home screaming. She was babbling on about murder, but no one could make head nor tails of what she was saying. One of the doctors sedated her and called the police. A notice was put out, but no one came forward to claim her as such. She was older than in your photo. When the police had gone the nurses put her to bed. She had a bag with her, one of those travelling carpet bags and when they opened it, they found it was full of money. Thousands of pounds and I mean thousands of pounds and a little notebook which had her name in it. The doctors decided they would use the money for her keep until she recovered, but she never did. Poor woman. She has just sat in her bed or chair since.'

She handed me back the photo and I asked the receptionist if I could see Mary Smith. The cook returned to the kitchen and I waited while the receptionist organised someone to escort me.

After a few minutes, an orderly arrived and told me to follow him. We took a lift to the next floor and at the end of the corridor he knocked on a door before opening it and going in.

'Mary, you have a visitor.' He looked to me and said, 'We think she could be about a hundred but it's only a guess.'

I stared at the woman in the chair. She was indeed very old and wrinkled. I called her name and she looked at me with the same cold eyes that had looked out from the photo. I held the photo in front of her and asked if it was her.

I was beginning to think she had not understood me when she took the photo from my hand and traced her bony finger over the face of the man.

'Horatio.' She paused. 'I put him in the shed you know?' she croaked.

I breathed a sigh of relief. I had found her, and she remembered.

Suddenly the door slammed shut. Mary's head jerked up and she began to scream. Looking around I saw two ghostly figures of girls holding bundles in their arms looking down at her. They began to float towards her. Mary screamed louder and then collapsed. The ghostly figures moved away but then the cat appeared. It jumped onto Mary's lap and scratched her face many times. The orderly and I were too stunned to move.

The door burst open, and a nurse ran in. The cat ran out. Mary didn't move.

I sank onto the bed trying to make sense of what I had seen, while the nurse checked for signs of life. Everyone's attention was on Mary when I noticed my ghostly girls fading away with smiles on their faces.

While everyone was busy, I quickly looked in the drawer and found the little notebook that had Mary's name in it. Slipping it into my pocket I edged away and left the room. The cat appeared at my feet and walked with me back to my car. I couldn't begin to try to understand how the cat came to be there or even why it had acted as it did.

Back home I poured myself a whisky and gulped it down.

My nerves were none the better from the events.

Remembering the notebook, I took it out and looked through it.

It was just a list of figures, money which I presumed related to what had been with her when she turned up at the home. No information about the girls or the man. What it did have was her maiden name Harris. She had written it at the back. Mary Smith nee Mary Patricia Harris.

I telephoned the police inspector and told him what I had discovered. He invited me to the station the following day to make a statement.

I sat at the kitchen table and put the notebook in front of me. What were my ghosts thinking now I wondered.

As if on cue I saw two chairs being pulled out from the table as my two girls made way to sit. The cat jumped up on my lap and I reached my hands out to the girls. They each took one and we sat there in peace. I told them all I had found out but somehow, I had the feeling they already knew.

A while later they were smiling and laughing as they left the room and headed upstairs followed by the cat.

Watching I was tempted to think about finding out who the cat was but for the moment I relaxed knowing that my ghosts and cat were happy and would be staying.

This story is dedicated to my friends in my diet/health group who enjoy the poems I write and encouraged me to go further with my writing. Thank you.